W9-BYC-927

Because You're Lucky

Hays ©97

Because You're Lucky

by Irene Smalls
Illustrated by Michael Hays

Little, Brown and Company
Boston New York London

For Dawn, Kevin Logan, and Jonathan
"I love you, black child"
—I.S.

For my cousin Carl
—M.H.

Also by Irene Smalls:

Irene and the Big, Fine Nickel
Jonathan and His Mommy
Louise's Gift
Irene Jennie and the Christmas Masquerade: The Johnkankus

First Edition

Library of Congress Cataloging-in-Publication Data

Smalls-Hector, Irene.
Because you're lucky / by Irene Smalls ; illustrated by Michael Hays. — 1st ed.
p. cm.
Summary: When Kevin comes to live at his cousin Jonathan's house, both boys must make some big adjustments.
ISBN 0-316-79867-3
[1. Family life — Fiction. 2. Cousins — Fiction. 3. Friendship — Fiction. 4. Afro-Americans — Fiction.]
I. Hays, Michael, ill. II. Title.
PZ7.S63915Be 1997
[E] — dc20 95-36023

10 9 8 7 6 5 4 3

IM

Printed in Singapore

The question traveled through the family like wildfire. Cousin Cheryl called Great-Aunt Myrtle, who called Nana Louise, who called her goddaughter Yvonne, who called her brother Jimmy, who called Aunt Laura. Who was going to take Hazel's boy, Kevin? Softhearted Aunt Laura was the first to say yes.

So caramel-colored Kevin with the long curly lashes came one day to live with his aunt Laura, her son, Jonathan, and her daughter, Dawn. He came without a toothbrush or a toy. He came without a change of clothes, and he came without a mommy or a daddy.

Tall, teenaged Dawn answered the door.

She eyed the tiny newcomer suspiciously. “Momma, how come that raggedy little boy has to come and live with us?” she complained to her mother after she had let him in.

“Because I’m his aunt and you and Jonathan are his cousins and he’s family. Family has to stick together,” her mother answered firmly.

“Hello, Cousin Kevin. How very nice it is to meet you. We’re delighted to have you come to stay with us,” Jonathan’s mother said loudly to Kevin.

“Hmmph,” Dawn sniffed. She brushed past Kevin and went into her room, closing the door behind her. A few minutes later, the door reopened. Dawn reached out and hung a sign on it: NO LITTLE BOYS ALLOWED.

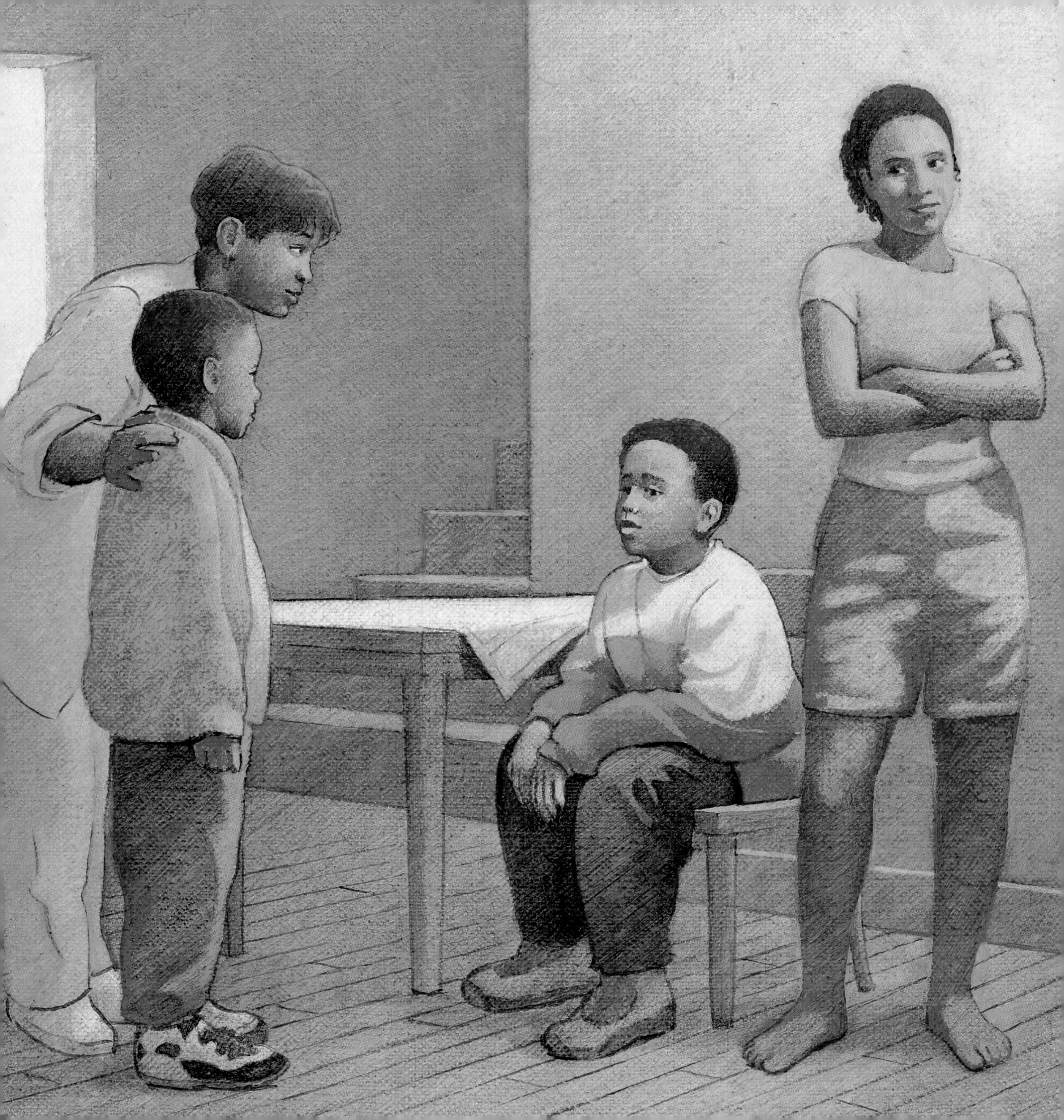

Kevin's large brown eyes opened wide as he stood very still and stared at the two strangers left in front of him. Hopeful, he looked at his aunt. "My name is Kevin Logan; my name is Kevin Logan," he sang softly to himself.

Jonathan frowned, his sturdy nut-brown body twisting away. "Why does he have to come to our house?"

"Because he has nowhere else to go," Jonathan's mother whispered through her teeth while smiling at Kevin.

"Well, I don't care. I want him to go away," Jonathan muttered.

"Remember you always said that you wanted a brother to play with?" Jonathan's mother said in a soft undertone, her hand on Jonathan's shoulder. "Kevin can be just like a brother to you."

"Yeah, I want a brother, but not him," mumbled Jonathan as he went upstairs to his room.

Kevin stared nervously at the floor. His hands clenched into fists.

"Never mind those two," Jonathan's mom said as she knelt and unbuttoned Kevin's jacket. She gave Kevin a big hug and led him into the kitchen. "They're just being difficult. They'll come around. You're family. I'm so glad you've come," she chattered.

As she tied on her apron, she said, "I hope you like pancakes."

Kevin gobbled them all up.

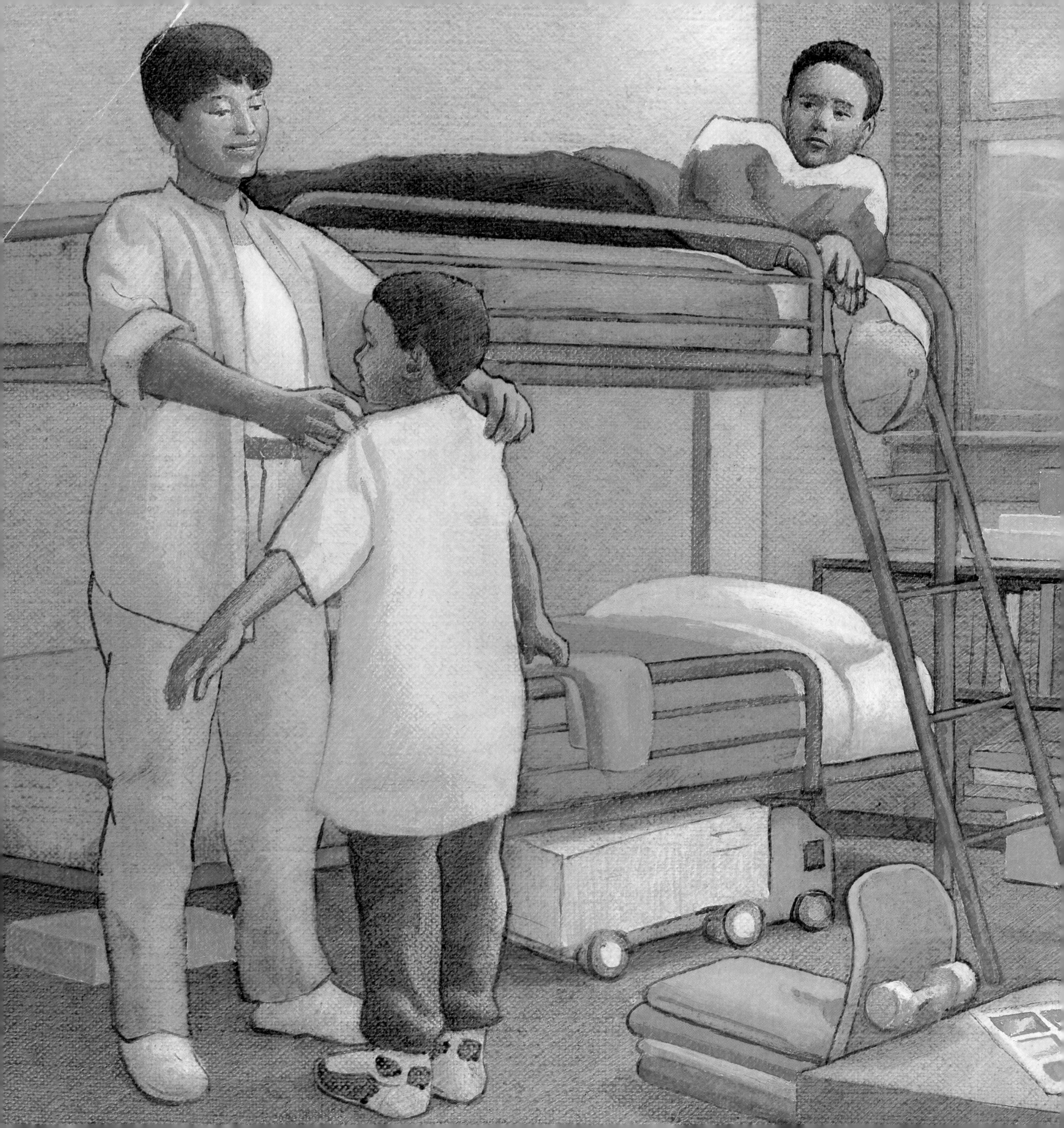

Then Jonathan's mom took Kevin upstairs. "This is where you'll sleep," she said, pushing aside a pile of clothes and toys, showing him into Jonathan's room.

"Yes, ma'am," Kevin murmured.

Jonathan peevishly peeked from his perch on the top bunk, his lips in a tight line.

Jonathan had so many clothes and so many toys. They spilled out of drawers, were scattered on the floor of the closet, stuck out from under the bed, and sprawled on top of the dresser. Jonathan's mother took half of Jonathan's clothes and shared them with Kevin.

Kevin stood awkwardly as Jonathan's mother tried one of Jonathan's shirts on him. "The clothes are a bit big, but you'll soon grow into them," Jonathan's mother said with a laugh and a soft pinch of Kevin's cheek.

Jonathan exploded: "It's not fair! How come I have to share my clothes? How come he gets to sleep in my bunk bed?"

Jonathan's mother answered, "Because you're lucky. You have a home, a family, so many things, and so much love. You're lucky that you have so much. You can easily share some of it."

Kevin tried to smile. "My name is Kevin Logan," he whispered. Jonathan didn't reply. Kevin started to whistle as though he didn't have a care in the world.

Jonathan's mother drew Kevin close to her and kissed him on the forehead. "Kevin, this is home now. Get settled in.

"I know that you'll be comfortable here soon," Jonathan's mother said as she left.

"Hmmpph," Jonathan groaned, glaring at Kevin. Jonathan hid under the covers and let Kevin settle his own self in as best he could.

5+2=7
8+3=11

The next day, Kevin went to Jonathan's school. "Hi, hi, my name is Kevin Logan," he sang out to the other kids. They smiled and wanted to be his friends. He made lots of friends but not with his books.

Kevin struggled with his writing. He grinned, and he struggled with his reading. "Sometimes I have a hard time, but I'll just keep trying," Kevin said to his teacher as he tried very hard to smile.

"Keep trying, Kevin. I know you will catch up," his teacher said encouragingly.

At home Jonathan, who was in the smartest class at school and easily aced all his tests, whined to his mother, "Everybody likes Kevin. Nobody likes me. Nobody. I'm stupid."

Jonathan's mother said, "You're not stupid. Lots of people like you. Don't be jealous. You are wonderful, and you're very lucky."

The two boys had birthdays a month apart. For his birthday, Kevin got a whole set of spacemen. At first Jonathan didn't want to play. Jonathan said that spacemen were dumb. Kevin laughed. Jonathan watched him play space games. He seemed to be having such fun that one day Jonathan started to play, too.

On his birthday, Jonathan got a chess set. He taught Kevin how to play chess. The boys would play and play.

Jonathan showed Kevin around the public library and taught him how to use the family's computer. Kevin showed Jonathan how to play football and how to make his special spaghetti sauce with ketchup.

Some days Kevin and Jonathan were friends, and some days they were not. Kevin had street-smart jokes and fight in his words as well as in his fists. Sometimes at night in the room they shared, Kevin would tease Jonathan. Jonathan would get angry, and they would fight.

"He hit me first," Jonathan yelled one night when his mother came in.

"He hit me first," Kevin screamed.

Jonathan's mother was confused. She couldn't tell who had hit whom first. So she said, "You both sit down quietly, and don't get up until you both say, 'I'm sorry.'"

Jonathan said, "You always believe Kevin. You don't believe me. You're my mother. Not his. I hate Kevin."

Kevin grabbed his own mother's picture off the dresser and started to run downstairs.

"Wait a minute," Jonathan's mother said. "Jonathan, I'm your mother, and I will always be your mother. Kevin wasn't mine before, but he's mine now. I have enough love for all of you. Now, both of you go to sleep."

One day after another shoving match, Kevin packed up his half of Jonathan's clothes and moved across the hall to the guest room.

Jonathan hollered, "Get out and stay out!" as Kevin left.

"He made me mad — that's why I left him," Kevin said to Jonathan's mother.

That night Kevin went to sleep in his new room in a wink, but Jonathan had trouble going to sleep. It had been a long while since he had slept in his room all by himself.

The next day was Saturday, and Jonathan watched cartoons for a long time because it's hard playing chess all by yourself. Kevin stayed in his room all morning.

"Where's Kevin?" Jonathan asked when his mother went into the living room.

"Oh, he's up in his room, I guess," Jonathan's mother said.

"Where's Jonathan?" Kevin asked when she went upstairs with the laundry.

"Oh, in the house somewhere. I think he's looking for you," Jonathan's mother said.

When Kevin came down, he looked around. Then he stuck his head into the living room.

"That you, Kevin?" Jonathan shouted.

"Yep," Kevin yelled back.

Kevin and Jonathan both said "Sorry" at the same time.

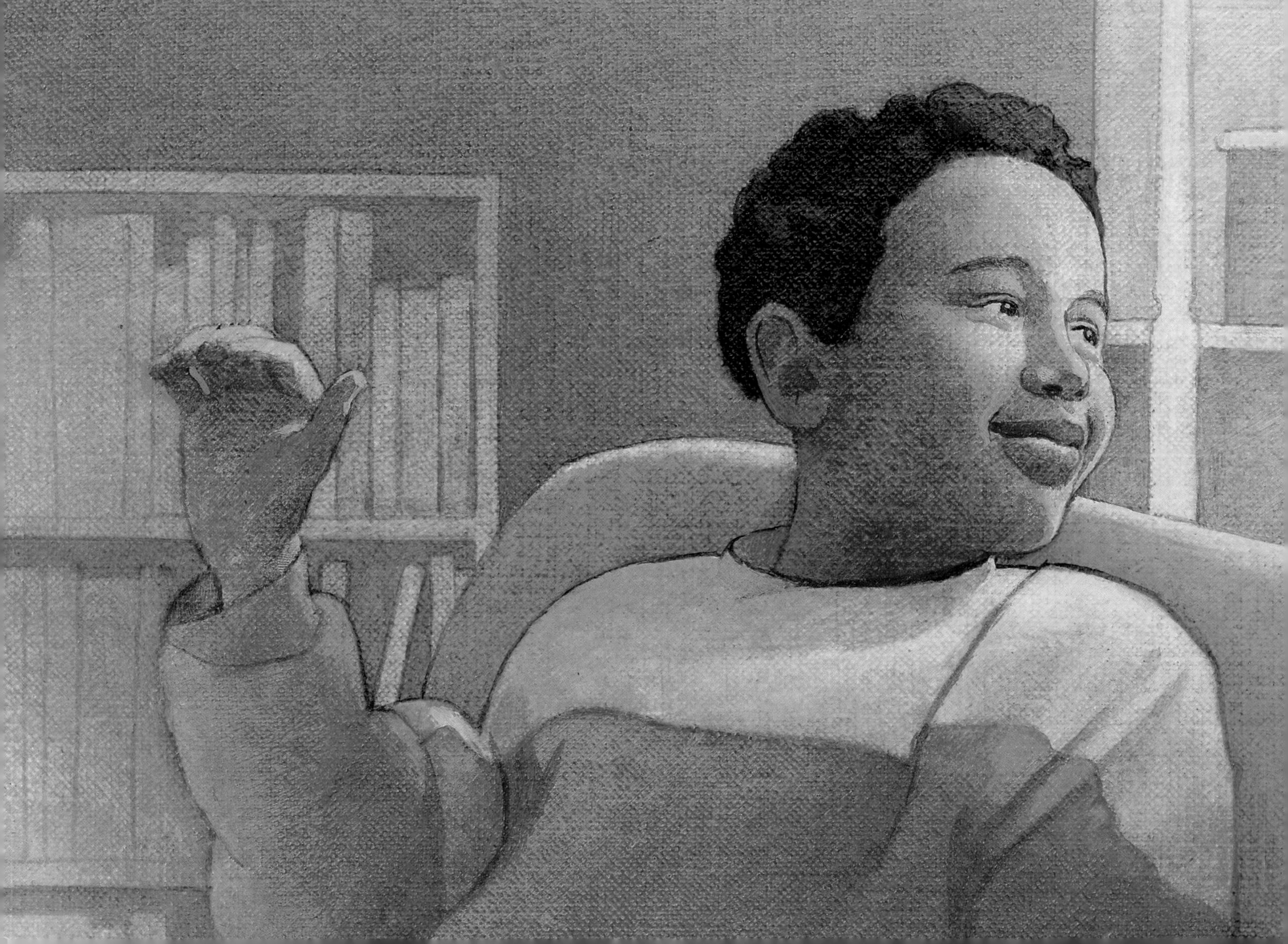

There was a short silence. Then Jonathan asked, "Do you want to go to the park?"

"Yep, yep, yep!" Kevin answered, so quickly that they both giggled.

Kevin and Jonathan went to the park. They came home when it got dark.

Jonathan's mother, standing at the door, announced, "Supper and then bedtime."

"So fast?" Kevin asked.

"We're having fun! Why do we have to go to bed now?" Jonathan asked.

Jonathan's mother smiled at both of them and said, "Because you're lucky."